SIN CITY ANGELS

BY

C.S Anderson

Alucard Press

Chapter One

Nobody notices when the Angel walks into the bar.

For the record nobody usually does.

Except for folks like me, I am what is called, a Dabbler. Half human, half Warlock and as far as my father is concerned, a one hundred percent unwelcome embarrassment. I am stronger than I used to be, but even at my weakest, I had enough magic in me to recognize Seraphim when they walk right by me.

Which thankfully, the Angel does, ignoring me completely. It is clearly on business of its own, so I go back to minding my own.

To be on the safe side, I should probably get up and leave and find somewhere else to drink, so there is no risk of me getting tangled up in whatever business it is here on, but fuck it.

It is raining outside and I was here first.

Can't help wondering why it is here though, this is at best a working man's bar and at worst a complete dive, with a mostly human clientele. A couple of Weres are drinking boiler makers at the other end of the bar, studiously ignoring me. They would likely, cheerfully drag me out into the alley behind the bar and tear my guts out, but for the moment I am under the protection of The Council, so they pretend they don't see me. I set a Packmaster on fire a little while back and while these two aren't from that pack, that little stunt has made me really unpopular amongst the occasionally furry set.

Other than them, the Angel and myself, everybody else in the bar is human or so skilled at passing as human, that I can't tell the difference.

When Angels interact with humans, they tend to do so amongst the rich and powerful so they can influence their choices and exert a measure of control in how things play out. I have only run into a few of them here in Sin City and like now, they have ignored me completely.

I am so ok with that.

I just barely survived my last brush with my fellow Sub Rosa, which is just the fancy name of all the various and sundry supernatural mythical types that call Vegas home. My surviving ended up depending on a deal my lady love made with Lucifer.

Still haven't found out what the price tag on that is going to be.

The Angel sits down at a table in the back, this one has taken the form of a large black middle aged bald man. If I squint, I can get a glimpse of the wings it is hiding behind carefully constructed glamour. It sits down with a sense of patience that tells me it is prepared to sit there for decades, if circumstance call for it to wait that long.

Waiting for what, I can't help wondering.

The cell phone in my pocket buzzes, it is the fifth one that I have had this year. The magic in me is enough to play havoc with electrical devices, because I am basically untrained. I don't know enough to shield it, so I keep shorting the damn things out.

"Hello." I bark into it, as I signal the bartender to bring me another pint of my current favorite IPA.

There is a hissing jumble of static with a weird warbling tone behind it and then there is only Genevieve's panic stricken voice.

"Run Robert Jones! Wherever you are run for your life!"

Then the phone bursts into flames and cursing, I let it fall to the floor.

"What the hell man!" The bartender shouts at me from the far end of the bar, I give him a half assed apologetic shrug and stomp the fire out.

No idea what has Genevieve so wound up, but I am at least smart enough to know that she wouldn't tell me to run for my life, unless there was a damn good reason.

I throw some money on the bar to settle my tab and prepare to get the fuck out of Dodge.

That's when an Imp walks in carrying a briefcase.

Curiosity killed the cat and all that and I am pretty sure some day it is going to be the death of me, because I don't run like I am supposed to. Instead I watch as the grimy little prick walks straight up to the Angel and puts the briefcase down on the table in front of him. He then bows deeply and turns on his heel and leaves the bar.

The Angel stares at the case with an unreadable expression for a long moment and then he opens it. As he reaches into it, a pulse generates from him, freezing all of us in the bar in place. It's as if time has somehow thickened and congealed and we are stuck in it, like flies in amber. From the briefcase he draws a large handgun.

He stands up, the next sound is the sound of him clicking the safety off.

That sound seems to break the spell holding us frozen in time, sound comes rushing back in and with a slight lurching sensation, time starts up again.

Then he opens fire and the room dissolves into screams and chaos.

It is a new part of the landscape in this country and is becoming just as American as baseball and fucking apple pie.

We have us an active shooter situation.

Yeah.

I totally should have run away when I had the chance.

Chapter Two

Instinctively I throw up a protection spell and a few stray bullets rattle off of it harmlessly, their energy spent, they fall to the dirty bar floor.

The humans around me aren't so lucky.

The Weres, to give their furry asses credit, step up and take some rounds for the team, stepping between the demented Angel and the humans in harms way. They twitch and jerk with the impact of the bullets, but since they aren't silver, they are healing before the scared tourists they are protecting have even run screaming from the bar. The council will thank them later, letting tourists get splattered across a bar full of other tourists is, generally speaking, the one buzzphraze that gets their damn attention.

Bad for business.

A fifty something blonde woman in a pink pantsuit catches one right between the eyes and a hot spray of blood and chunks of things worse than blood splatters me.

Ok, now I am pissed off.

I should be terrified, but as my dear old daddy used to tell me, I am just not smart enough to be afraid of anything. So, I gather every scrap of magic I can muster to me.

The Angel is beyond my power to hurt with my limited magic. Hell, it would be beyond the strongest Warlock's power to do any real harm to him.

But the floor it is standing on and the ceiling above it...

Well, that is a whole other fucking story.

As is the gun in its hand.

I take a deep breath and fling out the strongest shattering spell that I have ever done, it is aimed at the floor, the ceiling and the gun.

Yeah, precision isn't really my stock and trade.

My friend Marcus recently used a power he, strictly speaking, isn't supposed to have to increase my own little reserve of magic, but the results of my spell surprises even me.

The gun explodes in his hand, as the floor below him gives way, as a big ass chunk of ceiling comes down on his head.

The Council's spin doctors will convince the media that it was a terrorist attack and that the sole suspect died when he detonated his suicide bomb vest.

There will not be a single body recovered from beneath the rubble. I sent out a pulse of seeker magic and the Angel has already taken its leave of this earthly plane.

Sirens begin to wail in the distance and the sound blends into the chaotic mix of screams from the terrified and wounded. The first responders will have their hands full when they get here.

I need to be somewhere else entirely when they arrive.

Pulling off my bloody hoody, I toss it aside and grab a leather jacket hanging off the back of a stool on the way out the door. Its owner is either dead on the floor or is lucky enough to have trampled their way out the back door.

Lucifer is leaning against the dumpster in the alley when I spill out into it, along with some seriously panicked humans. Once again he is in the form of a raven haired, young Japanese school girl and is chewing a big wad of bubble gum. I tend to think of him as male, no matter what form he decides to take and I am never all that happy to see him.

"Evening Dabbler." He greets me politely in a bored tone.

And then he is gone, like he was never there in the first damn place.

No time to waste worrying about it now, I need to put some distance between me and the bar, pronto! I am not even a block away before the place is totally engulfed in flames.

As I walk away, I try to wrap my head around the madness that just happened, Angels work quietly behind the scenes of human affairs. A whisper here, a slight nudge there, to influence things towards whatever their secret agendas are. They rarely intervene directly in events and to my knowledge, have never gone on a bloody damn rampage in a seedy dive bar before. It makes no damn sense, serves no conceivable purpose.

I need to get home and let Genevieve know that I am safe, and to ask her just how the hell she knew that I was in danger. She is a unique being, a water nymph who escaped a very powerful spell, binding her to a specific place, saved my ass and then took up residence in the body of a slain Succubus, through a deal of some sorts she made with Lucifer.

A deal she has steadfastly refused to tell me the details of.

It is one of the very few things that we argue about.

Another one is me forgetting to put the toilet seat down, but I think that an undisclosed deal with the Lord of Hell, sort of trumps that.

In my own humble opinion, anyway.

I wear a brown knotted leather cord around my wrist, Marcus gave it to me with instructions of how to use it, in case I needed to contact him.

We haven't seen much of each other since the night his father tried to use us in a bizarre ritual out in the desert. The Council hauled his father away, swept a lot of dark secrets under the proverbial rug and promoted my friend Marcus to the head of his House, in place of his father, who is even now rotting in a cell somewhere.

Marcus lost one of his mothers that night, even as I gained the love of my life, things have been strained between us since then. Neither of us has any idea of how to fix things, so in typical guy fashion, we keep pretending that there isn't a problem.

Yeah, that's another thing Genevieve and I disagree on.

I hold the cord to my lips for a moment and whisper a single word into it, before tossing it into the shadows on the left side of me.

Moving off into the night, I walk away from the heat of the flames of the bar burning down and hopefully out of the reach of anyone who would like to talk to me about it.

Human cops or stranger things, I am not feeling chatty right now.

An old wound on my shoulder suddenly drives me to my knees, with a massive spasm of sheer pain. Blood soaks through my shirt as I struggle back to my feet.

A better place to die than on my knees, at least.

Four extremely attractive and well-dressed club goers, drift into a loose circle around me on the street. They don't say anything, but the pain in my arm tells me what, if not who, they are and what they want. They are.....

Fey.

I was grazed by one of their arrows during a narrow escape from The Great Hunt in the midst of our problems with rouge Wizards and their pet Weres, a while back. It never fully healed, as my friend Marcus had warned me, it would not.

He had also warned me that it would reopen and bleed in the presence of the Fey.

Which is something of a relief really, because at first glance, it seemed like I was going to be taken out by a boy band.

"Hey Wrong Direction, what up?" I ask as cheerfully as I can muster, with a sharp pain in my shoulder and blood running down my arm.

"We were advised that you think that you are funny." The tallest of them steps forward with a hint of a swagger. It marks him as the leader of this little band.

The other three don't speak or even move, they stand there like statues and simply stare at me as their leader moves to stand in front of me.

"You don't look like much." He tells me disdainfully as he gives me a long look up and down, a disappointed look on his male super model face. His skin is pale and his hair is ebony.

"Wait until we get to know each other better, then you can really experience the full level of let down." I tell him flatly.

All of them suddenly have long glass daggers clenched in their fists, I didn't see any of them draw them.

"You are marked by The Hunt, we were told to seek one such and bring him back to our realm for questioning." Their leader tells me blandly.

"No thanks, places to be, people to talk to and all that." I tell him brightly as I gather magic in, as discretely as I can.

"I am afraid that I will have to insist." The one who has done all the talking so far tells me politely enough.

Marcus did this little thing with my level of magic, but even with what he gave me, I am a little wiped from the huge spell I flung at the crazed Angel in the bar. I am a Dabbler, used to being outmatched and over powered. So, I know a few low level, but useful spells, that have meant the difference between living and dying while I was on the run from the death warrant Daddy dearest had once put on me.

Some of them are just plain fun.

Lucky for me, it has been raining, I gather the spell to me and cast it under my breath as I throw my hands up sharply over my head.

Mud hex!

Instantly all the puddles around me start to bubble and boil. A few seconds later, they all start to spew columns of stinking mud that come crashing down all around me.

Protected by the spell, none of it touches me.

The Fey boy band, isn't so lucky.

They are all knocked to the alley floor by the sheer weight of the mud cascading down of them, their fashionable clothing, ruined in seconds and their startling good looks obscured by dripping masks of dark foul mud.

I waste no time while they lie there stunned, by the time the first one struggles shakily back to his feet, I am blocks away and still running as fast as I can.

There is no time to waste patting myself on the back for my clever escape. The night has gone to shit on me, first the crazy ass Angel shooting up the bar and then Wrong Direction trying to snatch me up. I need to get home and make sure that my love is safe.

Not another damn thing matters.

Chapter Three

Nothing and nobody else makes a try for me and I make it to my apartment building in one piece, more or less. I lean against the wall of the deli across the street from my place and send the barest flicker of magic at the wards I have placed around my home.

When the flicker comes back to me telling me that all is well, I let out the breath I didn't even know that I was holding. Relief floods me, but even so, I decide to err on the side of caution and arm myself.

It has been that kind of night.

I wrap my knuckles sharply nine times on the newspaper box on the corner and say the required words. It opens with a metallic groan and instead of newspapers inside, there is a Springfield XDS 9mm and two extra magazines, loaded up with jacketed hollow points. I load the gun and stick it into the pocket of my pilfered leather jacket, the extra magazines go into another pocket.

As I cross the street it starts to rain again, the weather has been a little on the wet side for Vegas, since Genevieve emptied the entire reservoir feeding the water fountain display at the Bellagio, on the heads of some misbehaving Wizards. Something about what she did that night, seems to have changed the weather a little.

She pretends to have no idea what I am talking about, whenever I try to talk to her about most of the things that happened that night.

I dig out my keys as I double time it up the three flights of stairs to our place. All my wards are in place, but all my senses are on high alert. My wards are the best I can make, but then again I am just a Dabbler, somebody or something stronger than me could have found a way around them.

When I open the door Marcus is sitting with Genevieve at our scuffed up kitchen table, he flashes me a tired smile as I come in and she is up from the table and in my arms before I can even say anything.

"I thought I had lost you." She sobs into my neck.

"Fat chance." I whisper into her ear.

"Tell me everything." Marcus demands as he hands me a cold beer and opens one for himself as well.

So, I sit down and walk him through the weird shit fest that has been my life so far tonight, he listens intently without interrupting and when I am finished he leans back in his chair and shakes his head slowly.

"The Fey seeking you, I can wrap my head around at least, though why now is a valid question. We escaped The Hunt months ago and you haven't exactly been in hiding. The insane part of course, is the Angel shooting up the bar, it is literally, I am almost sure, unprecedented. I will have my house historians go over the records, but I really don't think they will find anything. What was to be gained from such a spectacle? The Seraphim don't need guns, he could have killed all of the people in the bar with a wave of his hand. He could have wiped the place out of existence with a small shrug of power, why the gun?" Marcus sounds baffled, which makes me very nervous, because he is one of the smartest people I know.

I was sort of counting on him having a few answers, instead of more questions.

"We should go see the Librarian." Genevieve says as she opens a bottle of water and guzzles the whole thing down.

Marcus and I exchange a quick look, it isn't a terrible idea. If anyone has a record of something like the Angel attack happening before, Chris Haney would be the guy. Local Sub Rosa call him the Librarian.

"Now might be a good time." He tells me, he stands up and pulls power to him, I can feel the tingle of it on my skin. It is like standing a little too close to a lightning strike, all of the hairs on my body standing up at attention. When he does things like this, it is a reminder that he is a full fledged Wizard from a powerful house of Wizards and I am just a half breed Dabbler.

I give him a nod as I grab Genevieve's hand and then take hold of his. I hear her give a little gasp as the translocation spell washes over us.

The ride is actually pretty smooth this time, I am only a little nauseous as we appear in front of a derelict looking building a few blocks off of the south end of the strip.

My lady love however is busy losing her lunch behind a dumpster she has lurched behind. She, to my knowledge, has never traveled like this before.

"I will walk back home, thank you very much." She says shakily as she staggers over and leans against me.

To my credit, I manage not to laugh.

Not that any of this is funny really, we have all lived in a little bubble of peace for the past few months and now that bubble has popped.

Marcus stands next to me seething with magic and trying like always to look everywhere at once. He gives my love a concerned glance that I appreciate more than I could ever tell him, the three of us form up and walk across the street to the dumpy looking used book store that is a Sub Rosa front. There is actually a ward to prevent curious humans from coming into the place. Anyone who might try to wander in will be beset by, what we shall call it, an emergency of the bathroom nature.

Here we will find the Librarian.

He will be here because he never leaves the store. Why? Well, because he can't, he had the misfortune to attract the romantic attention of a Necromancer, who did not take at all kindly to being rejected by him. She turned him into a shambling undead zombie, with an unhealthy appetite for human flesh. His mentor, the owner of the bookstore, being a powerful Wizard himself, did his best to undo the spell, but in the end that only meant that Chris got to be alive and human on the premises of the store. Two steps out the door and he is a rotting corpse, mumbling the word brains a lot.

His mentor has pretty much handed over the running of the store to him and it serves its purpose as a clearinghouse of information for our community. Chris can research and find answers for almost any paranormal question brought to him, this has earned him the nickname of, the Librarian.

A small bell above the door chimes as we open the door and step into the store, which once we are all inside, is at least three times as big as is possible from the size of the building it is in.

You Doctor Who fans know what I am talking about.

"Figured I would be seeing you sooner or later." Chris tells me as we walk up, he is on the phone and holds up a finger asking for a moment to finish the call.

"For the last time lady, there is no such thing as the unauthorized biography of Dark Molly! Why? Well, I suppose because the crazy bitch would gut anyone stupid enough to try writing one, that's why!" He hangs up the old fashion clunky black desk phone, shaking his head ruefully.

"I know what happened, I have no explanation for it at all. I have clerks combing the records in back, but I doubt that they will find mention of anything like what happened tonight." He tells us tersely.

"Librarian, I know you don't have answers for us, but any theories? Any thoughts at all on what could be going on here?" Marcus asks him in a formal tone, throwing the weight of his House behind the question.

Chris sits down in the overstuffed leather chair behind his desk, sighing heavily. He sketches a privacy charm in the air in front of him and the rest of store that had been, moments before, bustling with patrons and clerks, falls silent as a bubble of magic separates us from them.

"Random ideas? Lucifer is in town, which always tosses a wild card into the mix of things. Your lady's stunt with the fountains, threw a monkey wrench into the balance of magics around here and that balance is still struggling to restore itself. Rumors are circulating that the Goblins are close to perfecting whatever they have been building since just about the beginning of time and they have become more secretive than ever. Not to mention the ritual that almost happened out in the desert a few months ago."

Marcus gives him a hard stare.

Chris gives him a smartass smirk.

"Yeah, I know, it never officially happened and you have no idea what I am talking about. I hear everything eventually oh impressive head of major House, secret or not. I have a lot of time on my hands. You might have heard by now, I don't get out much." Chris tells him with a shrug and a note of bitterness in his voice.

"Of course, Librarian. Please continue." Marcus tells him with an apologetic smile and a slight bow.

"As I was saying, magically things have been unsettled lately, but none of that explains what happened with the Angel tonight. I haven't the beginnings of a clue as to what to tell you past that." He says with a shrug.

A thought occurs to me that probably should have before, in my own defense, I have been a little preoccupied trying to stay alive and not getting kidnapped by the Fey tonight.

"How did you know I was in danger?" I ask Genevieve.

She holds out a hand to me and says something lilting under her breath and a glowing red line slowly arches from her chest to mine. It is beautiful, pulsing in time to our heartbeats.

"Because our hearts are connected Robert Jones." She says simply.

"Oh for crap sakes guys, get a freaking room." Chris groans as he waves the privacy charm away.

Chapter Four

A slender attractive witch with closely cropped dark hair, wearing a thread worn Rolling Stones t-shirt and a silver ring in her nose, comes up and whispers something into Chris's ear, while handing him a small scroll. A look of surprise flashes across his face so fast that I am not even sure I saw it in the first place. He excuses himself and goes with her towards the back of the store leaving us standing there.

Before we have a chance to even ask each other what the hell that was all about, the bell above the door chimes. A tall, pale, cadaverous looking figure in an immaculate chauffeur's uniform steps into the store and looks around. A ghastly smile stretches across his angular face as he sees us.

"Greetings, kind folk. I come bearing a message from my Master." He tells us with a low stiff bow.

Beside me Genevieve gasps and grabs my hand and squeezes it so tightly that if I wasn't so damn manly, it might even hurt. I glance over at her and see that she has gone pale and her face looks stricken.

I put myself between my love and the damn ghoul that just walked in and in the words of a good Vampire friend of mine, I put on my best bitch face.

"Not another step closer Chumley." I tell him quietly, but with all the edge I can manage.

Grinning, he takes another small step.

Marcus smoothly moves to stand next to me and I can feel him gathering in his considerable power, I do the same, with what I have to work with.

Chumley just stands there looking at us for a long moment, he is the servant of the being known as Lucifer and is temporarily on this plane of reality while the spark of his Master inhabits the host he is using this visit.

"No need for alarm, good folk. I am merely here to hand deliver a message from those my Master used to stand with. He is doing them the courtesy of having it delivered, for what we might as well call, old times sake." His voice, as always, leaves me feeling stained for hearing it. He snaps his fingers and a folded piece of paper floats from him to hover just in front of Marcus.

He snatches it out of the air and without glancing at it, stuffs it into the pocket of his suit coat.

"Message delivered. Now, be gone." Marcus tells him in a bored tone as he jabs a finger at the door.

"I am not sure that I appreciate your tone good sir." Chumley tells him after staring at us for a long moment. His head is slightly tilted and a slow build up of energy seems to be swirling around him. As it slowly builds, a mocking smile creeps onto his pallid face.

He licks his thin lips with an obscenely long black tongue.

For the record, yeah the damn slimy thing is forked.

Chris comes walking up, looking pissed off and as he comes he is chanting in a language that nobody has offered to teach my Dabbler ass yet. The Witch he left with, walks a couple of steps behind him, her hands busily sketching runes into the air as they come.

"Read the sign asshole, management reserves the right to refuse service to anyone. Consider yourself refused." He says as he claps both hands together releasing a wave of magic.

The front door opens itself wide and our ghoulish pal Chumley is flung backwards through it.

Jerk has the nerve to wave at us as he goes. The door slams itself shut.

"You three may leave by the service entrance in the back, simply state your destination and step through it. If I find anything out, I will be in touch through the usual channels." He tells us firmly while he stares at the closed door with a grim expression on his face.

I give him a nod as we walk by, as a way of apologizing for the trouble that we brought to his doorstep. He smiles back and gives me a thumbs up, then goes back to staring at the door, like he expects bad news to come through it.

In our world, opportunity may knock, but trouble just kicks the damn door in.

Marcus and I hustle Genevieve to the back of the store and find the service entrance.

"Home!" I shout as I give the crashbar on the door a swift kick and there is a soul numbing moment of absolute cold and darkness as we cross the threshold.

And then the three of us are standing in our postage stamp sized living room. Shakily Genevieve lowers herself into a chair and I can tell that she is fighting tears.

Marcus has been my friend for a very long time, no matter what factors may strain that friendship, now I know that he is still my friend by the simple kindness he shows my love.

He kneels beside her and takes her small hands in his and kisses them lightly, before touching her briefly on her shoulder.

"No need for fear, you are being protected by the Abbott and Costello of the magical world." He tells her with his patented roguish grin.

Her laughter relieves the tension in the room, like the safety valve on a overheated steam engine.

I am not laughing because of the worried look he gives me over her shoulder.

She wipes her eyes and tells us that she is going to go take a shower.

It has to be her fourth one of the day.

We sit quietly at my battered table until we hear the water running and her humming some pop song off key and loudly.

And then he takes the message out of his pocket. He reads it with an intent look on his male model face and sighing heavily he hands it to me.

I don't have warm fuzzy feelings that it is going to be good news.

Chapter Five

The message on the card is simple, basically the pleasure of your company is requested to discuss mutually important matters tomorrow at breakfast. It mentions both myself and Marcus by name and provides a time and a place for the meeting.

What isn't simple about it, is the way the note is signed.

A golden rune is seared into the heavy cardstock, a human looking at it would see a fancy design, but to us the mark seethes with a fraction of the power of those who placed it there.

It is the symbol of the Seraphim.

"Well, I hope they have decent waffles." I tell Marcus as I hand the card back to him.

For the record, he doesn't laugh.

"This has to be about what happened with the Angel in the bar, you were a witness, so I suppose it makes sense that they would want to talk to you." Marcus says slowly, I can almost see the wheels spinning in his head as he works things out in that big brain of his.

"Hopefully they aren't pissed that I pretty much dropped a ton of rubble on their boy, probably even dented his halo a bit." I tell him as I snag another beer from the fridge.

He waves the idea away.

"Nothing you, or myself for that matter, did, could actually do one of their kind any real harm. If they were angry they could just will you out of existence, no offense, but it is weird that they would pay a lowly creature such as yourself any notice."

Yeah, Angels are the all time gold medal rock star level winners at the whole being a snob bit. Their disdain for their bosses favorite creation, hasn't faded over the centuries, since their big guy went out for a pack of cigarettes or something and failed to come back. Humans are basically just hairless talking monkeys to them and they don't hold us Sub Rosa types in much higher regard.

"They must want something from us, it is the only answer that makes any sense, but what could they possibly want?" Marcus asks the question out loud, but I am pretty sure that he isn't expecting an answer from me.

"So we talk to them and find out what it is." I tell him as I hand him a bottle of beer.

"Actually, they won't be talking to us. Normal human's heads would pretty much explode at the sound of an Angels voice, us, well we would fall to the floor writhing in agony for a little while and then our heads would explode. They will speak to us through Puppets." He tells me absently, his voice taking on a vaguely lecturing tone.

I stifle an inappropriate laugh, can't help it, the idea of Angels sitting across from me with ventriloquists dummies on their laps is just too weird not to laugh at, but Marcus will get all pissy if I don't go through the motions of serious listening.

"Hey pal, let's play a game. Let's pretend that I don't know a single damn thing about Angels and what this meeting is going to be like." I tell him, I am still listening to the sound of the shower running in the bathroom. Lucky for us, she takes ridiculously long showers.

He sighs heavily and then nods. Getting up he begins to pace our tiny apartment as he gathers his thoughts. I know from experience that when he speaks his voice will be in lecture mode, which I hate, but I need to be brought the hell up to speed.

"Puppets, the Angels have always used them on the rare occasions that they have to meet with Sub Rosas like us. They are the souls of humans who are close to dying of some terminal illness. They will appear to us as what they looked like when they were young and healthy. The Angels will be touching one of their hands and will speak through them. Every word that they speak for the Angels costs them a few moments of life." Surprisingly his voice isn't clinical like he is giving a lecture, there are notes of sadness and other things that I can't quite define coloring it instead.

Well, that's a buzzkill.

"Are they forced to serve the Angels like this?" I ask him quietly, trying to wrap my head around what I am being told.

"No, it is entirely voluntary. They generally use humans who are very religious and by all reports serving in this way replaces any pain their bodies are feeling, with an ecstasy of sorts. Don't look at them during the meeting, it is a breach of protocol. Look at the Angels and if needed, direct your responses to them as well."

It goes without saying that we will be at the appointed place at the appointed time. Even my Dabbler ass knows better than to deliberately offend beings as powerful as the Seraphim. So, we go and see what they want with the likes of us and hopefully we survive the experience. There are no weapons we can bring with us, no spells that can really protect us and we have no bargaining chips in whatever game is being played.

The shower turns off in the bathroom, Marcus folds the paper back up and puts it in his pocket.

"I will pick you up in the morning." He tells me simply, giving my shoulder a squeeze as he walks past me and out the door.

I send a trickle of magic out to make sure that all of my wards are in place, they are as strong as I can make them. At the very least they should warn me of any danger that tries to cross them.

Of course, there are some dangers that are right here with me.

She comes out wrapped in one of my old faded, ratty bath towels and on her, it is more stunning than anything any runaway model has ever strutted down the fashion runway in.

"You thought Chumley was there to collect whatever it is that you owe his Master." I tell her quietly.

"Yes." She answers me in a small subdued voice and she is staring at the floor instead of meeting my eyes.

"Tell me what it is." I demand, trying hard not to let the anger I am feeling color my voice.

She shakes her head softly and moves away from me and into our small bedroom. I know better than to push, every time that I do she just shuts down and then we sit in awkward strained silence as we try to think of a way to find our way back to each other. Which we do by choosing to pretend that this debt isn't really hanging over us, which is getting harder to do all the time now.

"Marcus and I have a meeting in the morning. I am not sure what will happen at it, but no matter what you have to stand here inside of the wards ok?" I tell her firmly.

"With Lucifer?" She whispers, her eyes going huge and her lower lip starting to tremble.

"No, with some of his old buddies. We have been summoned to meet with some Angels. Absolutely no idea why, but they asked for the both of us by name." I keep my voice empty and casual.

I don't see her move, she does that sometimes, I am reminded that as normal as she appears, well, she isn't normal. That being said, one moment she is standing across the room from me and the next she is standing so close to me that I can feel the damp heat radiating from her skin.

She leans her head on my shoulder and I am undone, my love and need for her erases all rational thought. I should fight her and make her finally answer the question, that to be honest, is slowly poisoning things between us.

But instead, all I can think about is how much I want to kiss her.

So, that is exactly what I do.

You can probably connect the dots on what happens next.

Chapter Six

We pull into the parking lot of a popular mom and pop style breakfast place, called The Blueberry Hills Café. Something of an old Vegas instituton really. Think a fifties style joint, with crisply uniformed waitstaff, sporting big friendly smiles and an over all so wholesome it almost hurts, kind of ambience.

Marcus is dressed in a tailored black powersuit, that probably cost more than my current net worth, not that that is saying all that much. Me, well I am sporting faded tan cargo shorts and an old Grateful Dead tie dyed t-shirt.

It is hot out and despite the damn monkey suit my friend has on, it is my Dabbler ass that is sweating. The parking lot is about three quarters full, so it is going to be busy inside.

"Follow my lead, let me do most of the talking. Please, don't try to be funny." He tells me sternly.

"Hey, I will be on my best behavior." I promise in as sincere a tone as I can manage.

He doesn't look impressed.

Sighing, he turns his back on me and we start walking towards the main entrance of the café. He pauses at the door and I can sense him sending a small pulse of power ahead of us.

"They are here already, two of them." He tells me tersely over his shoulder and then he opens the door and we both step inside.

"Welcome to The Blueberry Hills! My name is Sophia. Just the two of you this morning?" A tiny blonde waitress chirps at us, in a voice that fucking screams, oh my god I am a morning person.

I am not a morning person.

Yeah, Marcus isn't either really.

But he gives her a powered down version of his flirty smile and her eyes go huge and her lips stretch into an even bigger smile. She falls all overself escorting us back to a table in the back, where two people are already seated.

They are a study in contrasts.

The woman is iceblond, pale as paper and thin as a rail. Her hair is pulled into a bun, so tight that it almost has to be painful. Her face is lean with knife slash cheek bones. Her eyes are the brightest shade of blue that I have ever seen. She is dressed head to toe in white. White long sleeved shirt, white jeans and white hightop sneakers. No jewelry, no make up. Her expression is one of vague disapproval as we come walking up. Every thing about her screams severeness.

The man is huge.

Like four hundred pounds of huge.

He is Japanese and built like a Sumo Wrestler. Bald as a fucking cueball and despite his size, dapper in an obviously tailored black suit. A massive watch, that once again, costs more than I have ever had in my bank account, is on his left wrist and there is a ruby the size of a dime, in his right ear. He is grinning like the cat that just ate the canary.

Which is disturbing, because to him, we might just seem like the damn canary.

Power radiates from both of them, like heat from an overworked radiator. I do the magical equivilant of squinting and yeah, I can just barely make out the hint of shining wings behind the human forms they are presenting.

We take a seat directly across from them and for a long moment, we all just look at each other.

"So, maybe you wouldn't mind clearing this up for us. Just how many of you guys can dance on the head of a pin?" I ask when the silence goes on for just a little too long for my mouth not to jump in and say something stupid.

Next to me Marcus sighs and does a classic face palm.

The male Angel's shoulders heave in a silent chuckle and he just shakes his head ruefully at me.

His girlfriend is less amused.

Her hand moves so fast, I never even see it coming as she reaches out and slaps me a hard one across my face.

My jaw shatters and shards of teeth erupt from my mouth in a hot spray of blood. The blow is so hard that my neck is violently twisted almost to the point of breaking. A shimmer of energy follows instantly behind the attack and all of the damage is fully healed leaving no trace, not even blood on the table cloth. I sit there for an instant with my ideas completely scattered.

Worse thing is, the bitch never answered my question.

"If we could perhaps get down to business?" Marcus suggests mildly tapping his fingers absently on the table top.

She glares at me for a moment, but then nods.

A pulse, just like the one the crazed Angel sent out in the bar before he opened fire, radiates out, freezing everyone in the restraraunt in place. Everyone, but us at the table, that is, and suddenly there are two more of us there.

Two young woman are suddenly just there, one on either side of each of the Angels. There is a sense of impossible duality to them, they are here and they are also elsewhere.

Part of my limitations of being, nothing but a lowly Dabbler, is that I don't know how to shield myself very well. I am picking up things from the pair of them, I wish that I could block out.

One of them is named Sheri Anne, the other is known as Gibbitt.

They are both here in front of me and in beds in separate hospitals hooked to tubes and wires and patiently going about the messy and lonely business of dying. Details flow into me despite the clumsy efforts I am making to block them, I am feeling a small share of their pain and sorrow. Sheri Anne is dying of some shit called Warner Syndrome, which means her body is withering away from a form of premature aging. Imagine being a vibrant spirit, trapped in a body rotting away from the inside out.

She appears to us as a beautiful lithe teenage girl, dressed in artfully torn jeans and a ridiculously oversized blue plaid shirt with silly ass shoulder pads. Her hair is teased to the point of being more or less bullied. A smart ass smirk lights up her face and neon green jelly shoes are on her tiny feet .

In another study in contrasts, the other puppet is named Gibbitt and there isn't a single damn silly thing about her. Instead of a smirk, her angular face is set in a fuck the world and leave me the hell alone mask. Her dark short hair is gelled up in short spikes and she is wearing a faded Queensryche t-shirt, a leather jacket, she probably kicked some bikers ass to get and scuffed up steel toed work boots. She looks a few hard lived years older than the puppet, but no more than twenty five or so.

She is dying of advanced Syphilis.

The energy I read from her is all but giving me the finger and daring me to judge and I know one thing about her instantly.

She has lived life her way, she has no fucking regrets.

Marcus touches my arm lightly and stealthily borrows me the strength and skill to sever the connection and I come back to myself to see the whole table staring at me.

"Sorry, let's get to it." I say wiping absently a tear running down my cheek and trying to keep my tone steady.

"Control your pathetic human emotions Dabbler, they are puppets nothing more. We summoned you here to discuss what happened with one of our bretheren the other night." Sheri Anne tells me as the female Angel lays a pale hand on her shoulder.

A grimace of pain flashes, like Summer sheet lightening, across the puppets face, as a reminder that every word spoken has its costs.

"Tell us everything." Gibbitt demands, as the male Angel touches her shoulder, I find myself respecting his economy of words. He probably doesn't give much more of a shit about what it is costing his puppet to relay the message, than his partner does, but is at least practical enough to choose his words carefully.

The words are not just words, there is a nudge of compulsion woven into them and I find myself spilling my guts. I tell them every single thing I can remember about the encounter with the crazed Angel, every impression, every random thought I have about what happened that night. I feel like a wet washcloth being wrung out by powerful hands until every drop of information has been squeezed out.

Finally it is over.

I sit at the table soaked in sweat and trying really fucking hard not to throw up on the nice clean table cloth. I glare at the male Angel, which is probably akin to a poodle glaring at a pit bull. He gives me a half ass grin and a small shrug of his shoulders.

"We came here to exchange information did we not? Your turn." Marcus says firmly and I can feel him amping up his own power so that he can appear as badass as possible. Think at least pissed off rat terrier versus pit bull.

Sadly that means he has withdrawn his shoring up of my strength and the connection between me and the puppets is back.

I swallow down a mouthful of bile and soldier the fuck on.

The Angels take their hands off of their Puppets for a moment and touch foreheads. As they do, there is a high pitched keening sound on the barest edges of our ability to perceive, that is quite simply awful to hear.

But at least it is very brief.

"No Warlock, we did not come here to exchange information. We summoned you and you came. You provided us with the service that we summoned you to provide, so you will, for at least the moment continue to exist. My advice? Don't push your luck." Sheri Anne tells us and through our connection I can feel what each and every damn word is costing her.

The male Angel puts his hand back on his Puppet's shoulder again and takes a deep breath as he prepares to defy his partner.

"I will tell you this, the Goblins are nearing the completion of what they call their "Great Machine." This seems to be sending out waves of power that is affecting some of our lesser bretheren. There have been a few such incidents and we are considering our response. You are advised to wash your hands of this matter, this is the only warning you will receive." Gibbitt tells us primly.

Marcus stares at the pair of them for a long moment and then shrugs his shoulders slightly.

"Are we done here then?" He asks putting as much of an edge into his deep voice as he dares.

The Angels both stand and I am pretty damn sure that the meeting is now over, until both Puppets reach out and pull them back down.

41

"No." Both Sheri Anne and Gibbitt say in unison.

Chapter Seven

The Angels both look totally startled, apparently the connection goes both ways and the Puppet has some limited freedom to act. Marcus looks just as freaked out as I am sure that I do.

"Our puppets each have something to say to you. This is unusual, but then again we live in unusual times. We will allow this." The female Angel says speaking through Sheri Anne.

I have a feeling that she isn't so much allowing it, as she simply can't somehow, despite all her power, prevent it.

"They will each be allowed to speak seven words to you, and then they will die." The male Angel tells us through Gibbitt.

Gibbitt stands up and stretches out one hand to grasp Marcus by the shoulder, being careful to keep the other on her Angel.

She looks him dead in the eye and draws in a deep breathe, no doubt the final one she will ever draw.

"I don't have a fuck to give."

With that, she simply vanishes. Through our shared connection, I hear her flatline in whatever hospital she is in. I can sense the staff rushing in shouting things like stat and code blue and so on.

But she is gone.

Sheri Anne smiles her smart ass grin at me, it contains more than a little regret, but it also contains a flame of hope of better things to come, that is the core of her faith, the faith that has kept alive, against all odds this long.

Keeping one hand on her Angel's shoulder, she manages to shuffle over close enough to me to whisper seven words into my ear.

And then she too is gone.

I sit at the table with my best friend and two fucking sterling examples of Seraphim and bawl my fucking eyes out.

Both Angels stand up and leave, the female one is glaring at the male one all the way out.

Nice to know that some things are just universal.

The pulse freezing the world in place ends and motion and sound flood back into the room. Everyone goes back to the business of talking and laughing and eating breakfast.

I stop crying and wipe my eyes with my sleeve.

Marcus and I sit in silence for a few minutes, until the waitress returns with a heated smile and a chirpy voice and hands us menus.

"So, waffles?" I ask Marcus.

"Why the hell not." He tells me with a sad wink and hands the menus back to the waitress.

Neither of us speaks while we wait for our food to arrive, we both just sit and process what just happened. I couldn't tell you how much time passed between when we ordered and when the waitress came back with our food. She managed to touch my friend, no less than four times while she dropped the food off.

We then sit in silence and eat the best damn waffles that I have ever tasted.

Strawberries, whipped cream, chocolate sprinkles, all that shit.

It helps ease the pain, but I think that I will carry the weight of what just happened, for a very long time.

Which, all things considered is ok.

Somethings should be remembered, no matter how painful that remembrance might be.

I close my eyes and cast my blessings, whatever they may or may not be worth, into the cosmos for Sheri Anne and Gibbitt.

Sheri Anne, may you rest in peace.

Gibbitt, kick ass in either Heaven or Hell.

Thinking it is going to be your choice.

Take no fucking prisoners either way.....

Chapter Eight

We eat our waffles, pay the bill and then get up and head for the front entrance. I shake my head as we walk, trying to clear my mind of the slowly ebbing input from the Puppets. I carry it as an almost physical weight, but that weight is slowly fading away.

No less than five waitresses and the hostess, more or less swarm my friend trying to give him their phone numbers as we try to walk out. He gives me a shit eating grin and an apologetic shrug and I decide to wait for him outside.

The moment I step outside, this turns into a bad idea.

As soon as I cross the threshold into the parking lot, the wound on my arm opens up telling me that I have unwanted company.

They move so fast, that by comparison I am a fucking oil painting.

A bag is shoved over my head, my hands are zip tied behind my back and I am unceremoniously shoved into the back of a white windowless van, that came screetching up in front of me, just before the bag went over my head.

Just like that, I have been taken and seconds later we are burning rubber out of the parking lot and then racing down the street.

Somebody kicks me damn hard upside the head, things go black for an instant and then I see stars.

"That is for my dry cleaning bill, you Dabbler fuck." One of the Fey tells me in a deep baritone.

Great, the same Fey posers from last night have found me.

Yeah, this is probably going to suck.

We drive in silence for maybe twenty minutes, one of the Fey, probably the bastard that kicked me, is pinning my head to the floor of the van, ungently with his booted foot. The van stops and rough hands pull me out of the van and force me first to stand and then to walk.

I hear a metal door screech open and I can actually feel it when we step out of my world and cross the barrier into the pocket realm of the Fey. Suddenly I can smell flowers and hear birds singing and I know from my last visit here, that we are in the forest leading up to the Fey nightclub Marcus brought me to.

Hopefully this visit goes a little smoother.

The bleeding from the wound I received from The Hunt has slowed, but I can still feel a thin trickle of it flowing down my arm. Pain from it throbs, keeping perfect time with my pulse.

One of them rips the bag off of my head and I find myself blinking in the sudden sunlight. Another of them cuts the zip ties off of my wrists with a glass edged dagger.

"Walk." Their leader barks giving me a little shove down the faint path winding down to the Crazy Horse.

So I walk, it is of course beautiful here. Now that my eyes have adjusted, the forest is a riot of color, every imaginable shade of green, even some unimaginable ones I suppose and wild flowers of all different colors. A fresh piney scent fills the air and as I breathe it deeply in, it seems to invigorate me a little.

"Dude, if you just send me the stupid dry cleaning bill, I will pay it." I offer with a grin.

"Shut up and walk. Not a complicated set of instructions." He tells me evenly with an unamused poker face.

A raven caws harshly at me from the top of a huge oak tree and all of them stop to stare up at it, like they have never seen one before.

It caws again and then flies off deep into the forest, I watch it go until I can't see it anymore.

They all four turn to glare at me.

"Yeah, yeah, I know, shut up and walk." I tell them and then I do just that. They form up around me and our happy little parade moves down the path.

No use trying to escape, they are all stronger and faster than me and I have no clue how to find the way out of this realm and back to my own. So, I go with these assholes and talk to whatever assholes sent these assholes looking for me and find out what the hell they want.

Which hopefully isn't my head on a stick.

"Well now, what's this? You bloody again? Didn't think you would show your scrawny ass around here again." The same Ogre that was working the door of the club during my last visit looks up at me and growls as we come into the club.

My guards push me right on by him, without sparing him a glance and without giving me a chance to explain that my scrawny ass was brought here against my will.

There is so much Fey magic pulsing around us, that I don't bother drawing my own to me. This isn't something that I will be able to hex my way out of, hell this isn't something Marcus could probably fight his way out of.

They shove me hard into a side room, before we make it to the main bar and I go skidding across the floor to land at the edge of a raised Dais.

"Welcome Robert Jones. You may address me as Villatonio and you may address her as Lilliante." A deep baritone voice booms out as I start to pull myself to my feet.

"Indeed, welcome, please have a seat." A husky contralto voice tells me in a sly amused tone.

On the Dais are two thrones, a man sits in one and a woman sits in the other. They are both Elder Fey and are dressed in the dyed green leathers that mark them as members of The Hunt. Each is also wearing a black cloak, fastened at the throat with copper broaches of some kind.

Being Fey, they are both impossibly attractive of course, but in a harder edged way than the younger Fey that brought me here. They have lived centuries longer and that experience has marked them in subtle ways.

They both stare unblinkingly at me for a long moment, waiting for me to obey her order and sit in the chair facing them.

"I would rather stand." I tell them politely.

She sighs dramaticly and waves her hand slightly.

The compulsion spell hits me and I twitch like a marionette with epilesy and lurch my way over to the chair and sit down so hard, that I am sure that my ass will have bruises later.

"Or maybe, I will sit after all." I tell her less politely.

"He doesn't look like much." He tells her in a skeptical tone, turning to look at her and ignoring me.

Yeah, never gets old hearing that line.

She shrugs without answering and sketches a rune in the air in front of her, hissing a few words under her breath as she does so. A trickle of her power, visiable as a glowing green thread, snakes out of her fingertips and touches the wound on my arm. It reopens it again and as the thread retreats, it brings a few drops of my blood back to her.

Sniffing at them, she flicks out her tounge daintily to taste them, an odd look crosses her face and she offers her companion a taste as well. He takes it and looks startled for a moment, before he turns his face back into a bored impassive mask.

Awkward really, sitting here watching them taste my blood.

"Um guys, this isn't really something I am into. Maybe you could take out like a Craigslist ad, you know Elder Fey into blood sniffing, seeking Dabbler for weird threesome? Just saying." I tell them weakly.

"You escaped The Hunt, not many can make that claim. You remain marked by it. One of our seers has made a prophecy that suggests one such as you, may figure into the troubles that come for all of us, for your realms and our own. Darkness approaches and we are desperately searching for any source of light to stand against it. Angels descend into madness, Lucifer walks your streets quietly chortling in glee at the mayhem to come and a race that none of us have paid close enough attention to, for far too long, have nearly completed their Great Machine." The woman Fey tells me grandly.

God, the Fey like the sound of their own voices way too much.

"Blah blah, winter is coming. The night is long and full of terrors and all that happy bullshit. I can pretty much guarantee that I ain't the chosen one you are looking for, people." I tell her.

Anger flashes across her face, she may not get the whole Game of Thrones reference, but she knows sarcasm and disrespect when she hears it.

She clenches her fist and I am suddenly consumed by pain, she doesn't break eye contact until several long moments of agony have gone by. At last she unclenches her fist and the torture ends.

"That being said Dabbler, you will remain here with us, until we have determined that very thing for ourselves."

Then they put their damn heads together and ignore me while they whisper back and forth to each other.

Like a couple of middle schoolers, in junior fucking high school.

Chapter Nine

After awhile, they stop whispering to each other and go back to staring intently at me. I think I liked it better when they were ignoring me. Their faces are unreadable, they should really consider going pro at poker or something, because it is like being stared at by living statues.

"Robert Jones, what did the Angel's Puppet whisper in your ear?" She asks me out of nowhere.

Now just how the hell did they know about that? Their henchmen grabbed me outside of the restaurant, there was no way they saw us way in the back, inside the restaurant.

"None of your business." I tell her flatly. Those words are a private matter to me, spoken at the cost of a life.

"That wasn't it, we know that it was seven words." She tells me with a puzzled tone to her voice.

Oh yeah, this is going to be fun.

"I mean that those words were spoken to me and I am disinclined to share them with you." I do my best to clarify it for her.

"We could encourage you to be more cooperative and forthcoming." She reminds me darkly.

"Why do you want to know? What possible difference could it make to you? While we are at how and why, were you spying on us?" Hoping maybe a few questions of my own will shift attention away from the idea of torturing me.

Always worth a shot.

She snaps her fingers and a largish spider floats down from the ceiling to dangle in front of my face, on a long strand of web.

"We have eyes and ears everywhere." She informs me with a graceful shrug of her shoulders. Another snap of her slender fingers and the damn thing scurries back up its strand of web.

I give a little shiver, I fucking hate spiders.

"Ok, that explains the how, but what about the why?" I demand, mostly to keep them talking instead of inflicting pain.

Sounds like a good plan to me.

They exchange a glance and then turn their attention back to me. When she answers, it is with more of a sarcastic tone than you would think a Fey Elder could manage.

"That is, as you say, none of your business."

There is a knock at the door and a Brownie comes in bearing a message scroll on a silver tray. They all look alike to me, but I suspect that she is the same one that waited on us the last time I was here.

Why do I suspect that?

All of the hands not holding the tray, are giving me the finger.

She bows deeply before Villatonio and offers him the message on the tray. He takes it and dismisses her with an absent wave of his hand, she wastes no time scurrying out, but gives me a wink as she goes by.

Villatonio reads the message intently and then hands it to her. She reads it and gives him a startled glance before carefully rebuilding her poker face.

"Curiouser and curiouser." She mutters under her breath, as she tosses the message into the air where it vanishes in a puff of smoke.

They both stand up and step off of the Dias to stand directly in front of me. Looming over and looking down at me with those damn empty expressions.

"We have been instructed to let you go, Robert Jones. We apologize for the inconvenience. You will be escorted to the door back to your world and you are free to go. Our business, is for the time being at least, concluded." Lilliante tells me in a formal tone.

"For realsies?" I ask wondering if it is ok to just stand up and start the whole leaving thing or if this is a trick of some kind.

Villatonio reaches down and pulls me, none too gently, to my feet, giving me a little shake before putting me back down.

"For realsies." He says with the hint of an edge to his voice.

And then they both just walk out of the room.

Leaving me standing there, wondering just what in the actual fuck is going on and not all that hopeful about getting any answers to that burning question.

The Ogre sticks his large head into the room and points at me impatiently.

"Well, come on then you big twat waffle, get a move on, I aint got all day. I am to walk you out and could your sorry ass please stay the fuck gone this time?"

Without waiting for me to answer, he turns around and leaves and I hustle to catch up with him, before anybody changes their mind about letting me go.

Which I pretty much worry about happening, every step of the long walk back to the door I got carried through earlier, but it doesn't .

In the end he just opens the door and waves me impatiently through it.

He does slam it a little harder, than strictly speaking, was polite, after I step through it though, but I try not to let it hurt my feelings.

Chapter Ten

Time runs differently between our world and the realm of The Fey, so I am not surprised to see that night has fallen as I come through the door the grumpy ass ogre just rushed me through.

I am just a little surprised to see Marcus standing there with a flaming magical sword though.

He looks surprised to see me alive.

All things considered, hell, I am a little surprised my damn self.

"You escaped?" He asks, frankly his dubious tone is just a little insulting. I mean, I didn't escape, but who is to say that such a feet was beyond me?

Well, just about everybody I suppose.

"No, they let me go." I tell him with a shrug.

The sword vanishes from his hand in a muted flash of light and a slight popping noise. He pulls out his cellphone and hits a speed dial number.

"I have him, he is ok. We are coming home." He says into it and then he puts it away.

"Thanks for the attempted rescue." I tell him reaching out to give his shoulder a quick squeeze.

He looks startled for a moment, but then a ragged tired grin flashes quickly across his face.

"Well brother, against all advice and my own best judgements, you are what amounts to my best friend. Of course I tried to rescue your dumb ass, but not with much luck, they strengthened the wards on their boundries to the point that I can't seem to breach them. Which doesn't give me a warm fuzzy feeling about how the Fey feel about the current state of our world." His voice has worried tones in it, that worry me.

My friend has considerable power and has been around a long time and isn't afraid of a whole hell of a lot of things.

When he worries, my Dabbler ass better worry a lot more.

There is a soft feminine giggle behind us, beneath the girlish sound is a dark chilling hint of the power inhabiting the being making it.

Lucifer.

"Evening boys! Hope I am not interrupting your little bromance?" Her voice is sly with the fallen Angels trademark, cruel amusement.

A slim Japanese schoolgirl stands under a streetlamp smiling at us, with one eyebrow arched. She winks and then launches herself into a series of cartwheels to land a few feet in front of us.

"Ta Da!" She shouts throwing her hands into the air.

"Fuck off." I tell her through clenched teeth.

Her eyes flash red for such a brief instant, that I could almost believe I imagined it, except for the equally brief spasm of pain that twists my belly into burning hot knots.

"Manners." She chides waving a delicate finger at me mockingly, the pain is gone, but we both know just how fast it can come back.

"What do you want?" Marcus asks politely, because he is and always has been smarter than me.

"Oh just to chat, catch up a little. We never hang out anymore." She tells us with a pout.

I know better than to ask the question burning in my mind, even as I struggle against the impulse to ask, I know that Lucifer won't answer and that he will delight in my weakness in even asking.

Yeah, that struggle against the impulse doesn't last long.

"What does she owe you? Tell me!" I demand and I am immediately ashamed of the desperate weakness in my own voice.

This earns me another waving of the finger and a softly muttered tsk tsk tsk, like an exasperated mother talking to a petulant, unruly child.

"That is between your lady love and I, my little Dabbler friend. No worries though, things are coming to a head nicely and that little tidbit of information shall be revealed sooner rather than later now."

Lucifer breathes a deep breathe and slowly lets it out again, a look of almost orgasmic pleasure ripples in obscene slow motion across the pretty young face he is wearing.

"I wish you could feel it, taste and smell it like I do. The coming tide of darkness I mean. Forces beyond your puny reckoning have brought us all to this point, vast games are being played out and one holds out hope that the balance has shifted and soon it will be a whole new playing field. Already it has begun, listen for a moment." He cups a hand to his ear and puts a finger to his lips.

Sirens fill the night, lots of sirens, even for a late night during peak tourist season in Vegas. Marcus and I exchange a startled glance, I can hear ambulances and firetrucks, as well as police cars.

They all seem to be racing to different places in the city.

As we listen they fade and normal sounds rush back in to fill the night again. Lucifer giggles obscenely again and turns her attention back to us.

"So you are here to gloat then? Doesn't seem like a valuable use of someone of your ranks time." Marcus puts as much scorn into his voice as he dares, just enough for the fallen Angel to hear, but perhaps not enough for him to take offense at.

"No, like I said, just catching up. You two have been busy little bees now haven't you? Meeting with Angels, consorting with the Fey. One wonders just what the Elders wanted with the likes of you, Robert Jones." She asks in a casual tone.

It would be smart to answer and just tell him the truth, that what they really wanted beats the shit out of me. Give up the few scraps of info about what happened that I have and hope he goes about his demonic business and leaves us the hell alone.

Yeah, that would be the smart thing.

But like my daddy always told me, I ain't smart enough to be afraid of anything.

"Well Lucy, old pal. That would be between me and them. No worries though, things are coming to a head nicely and that little tidbit of information shall be revealed sooner rather than later now."

Marcus sucks in a breath and I feel him pulling in power to come to my defense, I touch his sleeve and shake my head no at him. Lucifer and I spend a long tense moment just looking at each other.

A smirk steals slowly across his borrowed face and he does a litte odd half courtesy, half bow towards me.

"Well played Dabbler, well played. You continue to amaze and entertain me. In the spirit of that, I leave you both with a little parting gift of sorts."

She snaps her fingers and two pairs of Blues Brothers style dark glasses appear and float over to us. We both grab them out of the air at the same time.

"Put them on and look towards the heavens gentlemen." She tells us in a bright cheerful tone.

Then all amusement leaves her voice and we get a glimpse of that which lives within the shell that he is inhabiting.

Her eyes flash red again and a wave of very warm brimstone scented air hits us, the heat from it reddening our skin and the stench sending us into coughing fits. When she speaks again her voice has deepened and all but echoes with the power barely contained in it. The sidewalk that she is standing on cracks and begins to scorch and bubble.

"I think that you will find them a revelation."

With that she vanishes.

We stand there for a long moment looking at the glasses and then at each other and then at the glasses again.

"Well, this is probably going to suck." Marcus says grimly.

"No doubt." I tell him ruefully.

Marcus sighs and stares up at the sky for a minute before looking back at the glasses again.

"On three then? One..two..three." He says and then we both put on the glasses and look up as instructed.

The stars have all vanished from view, the night sky is a dark murky mess of dark clouds lit from within by smouldering shades of orange, yellow and red. There is just enough light to see what is flying through that night sky.

Flights of Angels silently and relentlessly circling high above Vegas, like vultures patiently circling a dying animal.

Most of them flying in neat precise formations, but some are following mad orbits of their own through the darkness above us.

One of those falls in a glowing arc towards the streets below and at that moment we hear a fresh wave of sirens.

"Fuck me gently with a chainsaw." I say outloud in a hushed tone.

Chapter Eleven

"You always did have a way with words." Marcus says tightly as he takes off the glasses and flings them away in disgust.

They vanish with a puff of nasty smelling smoke.

"Now what?" I ask quietly, still shaken by what we just got done looking at and struggling to come to terms with what it may mean.

"Bloody hell if I know brother, I need to wrap my head around this. But for now, I promised your lady that I would get you home in one piece and that is pretty much my goal for the rest of the night." He says with a shrug.

"I have beer at home." I offer with a weak grin.

"Always a solid beginning to any new plan." He gives me a weak grin right back at me.

Just then a huge wolf staggers out of a nearby alley. It has blood all over its muzzle that likely belongs to something else, but there is blood all over it, that is clearly its own.

It limps closer to us, strained whimpers coming from it, speaking of the pain that it is costing it to do so.

The wolf collaspes at our feet and goes into massive convuslison, signaling that it is trying to change back into its human form. A howl erupts from it, that slowly twists into the ugly sound of a very tough man screaming in unbearable pain.

Then Dominique, Packmaster of one of the bigger packs in Vegas is lying gasping for air and reaching up a gore soaked hand towards us imploringly.

"They are killing us, help…" He shrieks.

And then he passes out.

"Ok then, we may need a new plan." Marcus tells me solemnly pointing at the bleeding Packmaster.

"Keen observation there Sherlock." I tell him as I kneel down and check for a pulse on the Were, the one that held a deep burning undying hatred for me and had many times promised to tear me to bloody pieces and then eat those quivering pieces. Lately the only thing stopping him from making good that promise, was the no harm order that The Council had put out on me. This is the first time I have seen him since magically giving him a little shove into a bon fire, during what my lady love calls, the difficulties of a few months ago.

But not being a total asshole, I check for a pulse on the poor mauled bastard anyway.

He has one.

Not sure whether to put that particular piece of info into the good or bad news category.

"He has a pulse, we need to get him and us out of here." I tell Marcus looking up at him.

65

Marcus nods and then digs out his cellphone and hands it to me. Power flares around him as he begins a strong enough translocation spell to carry all of us back to my aparatment.

I hit the speed dial button and it only rings once before Genevieve picks up on the other end of the line.

"Guess whose coming to dinner love...?" I ask her and then the connection is broken as Marcus wraps us all up in the spell.

I cringe a little, because I know that this is going to be a bumpy ride.

Chapter Twelve

Genevieve gasps in some alchemy of pity and shock as she kneels down beside the torn up man, lying bleeding on her faded carpet. She wastes no time asking any questions and begins immediately tending to his wounds.

"Bring me water!" She commands and shaking off the nausea and dizziness from the translocation spell, I push myself off of the wall that was holding me up and lurch into the kitchen. Pulling open the fridge, I grasp a bottle from our supply of the dozens of them on the lower shelf and bring it to her.

She holds the bottle to her lips and whispers an incantation under her breath, the bottle is suddenly lit from within by a slight shimmer of golden light. A fresh scent, smelling like a waterfall on a hot summer day, fills the room.

The magic she is using is different from what Marcus and I are accustomed to, it is older, less organized and more primal. Elemental magic is powerful and capricious, the spell balances on a razor blade edge of helping or harming. Marcus gestures sharply and tries to nudge it in the direction we need it to go, with his magical strength.

I keep mine out of it, I don't have enough control to dare make things worse than they already are.

Raising the bottle high above her head, she whisper another incantation and pours the water all over her patient.

I watch as far more water than the bottle could of possibly held, splashes across the unconscious Were.

As I watch the water washes away all of the blood and his face slowly relaxes from the painful grimace he came in with. His ragged breathing smooths and becomes deeper, as he slips into a deep sleep. As we watch his wounds begin to heal and fade away.

"I need a shower." She tells us weakly as she stands up and goes into the bathroom.

"Did you know she could do that?" Marcus asks me quietly, staring at the Packmaster lying on our now soggy rug.

"No clue. Every single day brings new surprises." I tell him with a shrug of my shoulders.

Which is true, to all who see her walking with me down the strip, she seems like a pretty, young normal human female.

She isn't.

Once she was a water nymph, bound to the fountains at the Bellagio Hotel to keep the tourists entertained. She then used her considerable power to not only escape her bonds, but to rescue me from a really bad situation.

This is where is gets weird.

She then was transferred into the physical shell of a Succubus, more specificly, the shell of the Succubus that was Marcus's mother, well at least in a manner of speaking.

Did I leave out the part where she made a deal with the Devil to make some of this happen?

My bad.

Yeah, my life makes the most outrageous Jerry Springer episode look like a fucking Brady Bunch rerun.

All of that really just means that she isn't human, she is something else and we are still in the process of figuring out just what that something else means.

The shower starts up and that is our signal, we both grab a beer from the fridge and sit down. Both of us keeping a wary eye on our guest.

"Talk to me." He says simply as he settles into this chair and takes a long pull off of his bottle of beer.

So, I do.

I tell him everything I can remember from my encounter with the Fey, from the moment that they grabbed me up outside of the restaurant, to the moment I staggered out of the warehouse and back into our world. He doesn't interupt even once, he just listens and nods occasionally.

We sit in silence for a little while.

The kind of silence that two good friends can manage to sit in.

"I hate Fey Seers, it is all vauge psychic babble. It all tends to make sense long after what they predict actually happens. Them mentioning you playing a role in how things play out, doesn't mean that you are any kind of chosen one, or that it is any heroic thing you do. It could mean anything from you not eating cheese on some random Tuesday or what movie you decide to watch next, something that you do or don't do somehow ends up tilting the balance in some way." He tells me as he goes and grabs another beer.

Our guest growls in his sleep, but is still looking more or less harmless curled up in the fetal position on my floor. Scars, old and new criss cross his muscular frame, but he is looking less torn up by the moment.

When he wakes up, hopefully he can tell us what the hell is going on.

When he wakes up, hopefully he doesn't try and tear my guts out.

Pretty sure that I got the priority on that wrong.

Marcus feels it first, I can see the look of confused alarm cross his face as he turns and trys to take a couple of steps towards me.

I manage maybe a step towards him, before the full weight of the summoning spell from The Council gathers both of us in a nimbus of golden light, that builds towards a painful to look at crescendo, before winking out taking both of us with it.

Pretty sure the whole golden light thing is total bullshit and is just for dramatic effect, by the way.

True or not we are both gone by the time that my love turns off the shower and grabs for her towel.

That is the thing that I find that I am the most pissed off about, by the way.

I generally really like being there for that moment.

As most of you have probably figured out by now, it really sucks to be me sometimes.

The sound of the shower ending is the last thing that I hear, before the spell sweeps me into darkness.

Chapter Thirteen

The summoning spell doesn't dump us in The Council Hall as expected, instead we slam hard into the floor of the head of The Council's private chambers. The floor is cold marble, laid out in an intricate weaving of magical symbols, a depressing amount of which, I don't have the training to recognize. She is lying on a dark leather couch, dressed in a red silk kimono with similar patterns woven into it in gold thread.

Helena Regret arches a perfectly plucked eyebrow at us.

"Good evening gentlemen, thanks for stopping by." She greets us softly in her husky voice.

Marcus rises slowly, his fists tightly clenched by his sides as he struggles to control his temper. He is the head of a major house of Warlocks and is definitely not accustomed to being treated like this.

I am, so I get up just a little calmer than he does.

Not picking a fight with the single most powerful Sub Rosa in Vegas, falls right in line with my general survival plan.

"Calm yourself, Warlock. I apologize for the hasty and ungentle summoning, but this is off the official books and I was pressed for time. I had to act while The Council's attention was elsewhere briefly." She stands up as she speaks and there seems to be some sincereity in her mollifying tone.

He gives her a slow nod and unclenches his fists and dials down the power he was pulling to himself.

"Dabbler, your dance card has been pretty full lately. Odd that the pair of you keep ending up tangled up in events isn't it?" She turns her attention to me and there is hint of accusation in her voice.

"Odd and dreadfully inconvenient." I tell her with a shrug.

She speaks a word under her breath and her magic hits me like a sudden splash of cold water. It takes my breath away and for a moment all I can do is stand there as it works its way through me. It is an investigative spell and it is measuring me in countless ways for her.

The magic leaves me as suddenly as it hit and I stand there shivering a little from the after effects. She stands staring intently at me for a long moment, before gesturing towards a couple overstuffed chairs, that I swear weren't there a few seconds ago.

She seems subtly disappointed by whatever her reading spell showed her about me.

"Please sit, we have much to discuss and not a lot of time." She tells us as she sits back down on the couch facing us.

Marcus and I exchange a quick glance, he gives me a small shrug and we both decide to pretend that she was asking not telling us and we sit our asses down in the fancy chairs.

Even I can feel how deeply shielded and warded this room is, nothing said or done here will be detected by others. My paranoid side whispers that she can disappear us right here and now and nobody will ever know what happened to us. Marcus is somebody in our world and that fact might slow her down for a moment, but not if she decides it is really necessary.

"Forces are at work here that we don't fully understand, the Goblins have turned on some sort of dire machinery in their halls and it seems to be affecting the Seraphim to some degree. Lucifer walks the streets, all but chortling with evil glee, while rubbing his hands together and hints at carnage to come. I don't think he engineered what the Goblins are doing, but he is taking full advantage of it. The Fey whisper of prophecy that they don't even comprehend and even our very own Libarian can not make heads nor tails out of the whole mess." She paces before us restlessly while she talks, her body language screaming out the tension that isn't showing up in her voice.

"There is a wounded Werewolf in my apartment who says that an Angel was killing his pack." I tell her grimly as she walks by.

"We are aware of it, an Angel swooped down and somehow pulled the beast out of one of them and put it into himself, so he could and I quote 'become one of God's righteous wolves' end quote. He used the dying Were as a Puppet to announce that little tidbit. Other Angels hauled him away before he could do much more than slaughter a few Weres." She answers blandly as she continues to pace.

Pretty sure that the pack isn't as cavileer about the whole 'much more than slaughter a few Weres' bit, but she takes a bit larger view of things than most of us do.

"Why did you bring us here? Surely with all The Council's resources, you don't need us to tell you what is going on? If you have questions, then ask them, otherwise release us." Marcus demands.

"I wish I knew why I brought you here, truth be told, I simply followed a gut instinct that I needed to see you. To talk to you, to try and make some sense of all this madness. Something is coming, and unlike the unofficial slogan of Vegas, I don't think what happens here will stay here. I think the fate of the world is at stake." She snaps at him, her cool finally broken, giving us a glimpse at the desperate rawness of her need to understand what is happening. At her need to control and fix the problem.

The smart ass in me wants to scoff at her drama, fate of the world is at stake, sounds like a line from a bad campy horror flick.

Bad news folks, it has the simple ring of truth to it.

She stops pacing and sits back down on the couch facing us and gives us an expectant stare.

So, we sit and we tell her everything that has happened since the Angel went postal in the bar, in what seems an enternity ago now, so much has gone down since then. Marcus and I take turns talking and we interrupt each other to fill in any gaps in the narrative. We tell every damn thing that we know or even suspect about what is happening.

Bad news again folks, it ain't much.

She listens intently, only interrupting to softly ask the occasional clarifying question. When we are done, she stands abruptly and resumes pacing the room.

"None of that makes any sense whatsoever, I feel like a pawn in a game so massive that there is no hope trying to grasp the scope of it. I fear that it will come down to surviving what is to come and doing enough damage control that we can come back from the damage done. That is not a point of view I fear, that The Council will embrace. Even if I am the head of it." Her husky voice speaks of how unused to helplessness she really is.

Suddenly there is a loud and very insistent pounding at the door of her chambers.

Cursing under her breath in a language I don't know or even probably will ever speak, she gathers a banishing spell to her and without warning hurls it at us.

It sweeps both of us away in a wave of cold darkness and raw magical power.

Then it dumps us hard and dirty back onto the floor of my apartment and for a few seconds, we both just lie there stunned.

After I catch my breath, I notice a couple of things.

First thing is that the wounded Were is now sitting on my shabby couch dressed in the Star Wars pajamas my love bought me and that I have never worn.

For the record they are way too small for him and he looks ridiculous.

He also looks alarmed and is pointing a shaking finger in the directon of Genevieve, who is leaning against the kitchen wall holding her very swollen belly and panting softly.

Yeah, her looking extremely pregnant is the second thing that I noticed.

"Don't look at me Dabbler, I never saw this bitch before in my damn life! I just woke the hell up and she was like that!" Dominique tells me emphaticly.

Marcus struggles to his feet first and stumbles over to help me stand up as well and together we start to wobble over to her.

This has all the earmarks of being a very long and weird night.

Chapter Fourteen

Marcus flings a binding spell on our Werewolf guest, locking him to the couch, more securely than the strongest bong hit and then even as exhausted as he must be, manages to transport himself, myself and my suddenly quite pregnant girlfriend to the nearest form of help.

Us Sub Rosa types, don't have a lot of choices when we need medical care.

Being basically supernatural, is totally a pre existing condition.

Most of us are pretty damn durable, all things considered, but none of us are immune from harm in one form or another. When we are hurt we can't go to human doctors, so we rely on what we have available to us.

We go to a small underground walk-in clinic of sorts, staffed by Greg Smith and a handful of volunteers. He is an Alchemist slash hedge witch of sorts, truth be told, not a very good one.

Well, truth be told at least not a very reliable one.

Greg is kind of a fuck up.

Back in his day he used to work feverishly at the classic Alchemist task of turning lead into gold, after years of study and experimentation he managed to turn gold into lead, but in the process, did two quite unexpected things.

Thing one, was blow his workshop into damn smithereens.

Thing two, was to somehow in the process of that, become basically immortal.

He is well over eight hundred years old now, but looks like the same thirty something screw up he did back in the day. These days he drinks too much, smokes like a chimney, chases anything his unfocused eyes tell him is female and tends to the bumps and scrapes of our community.

As we walk in, he is busy extracting a silver bullet from a stocky Hispanic male Werewolf's hairy ass, with a pair of surgical tongs and an ungentle approach. We could hear wolf boy howling before we even hit the small dirty waiting room between us and the doc.

"Shut up you big baby! Next time keep it in your damn pants and don't get distracted when you know that a bounty hunter is tracking you. Your own damn fault it is." He tells his patient as he yanks the bloody bullet free, his Eastern European accent adding a guttural thickness to his speech.

Yeah, his bedside manner kind of sucks.

"What you want?" He snaps at Genevieve and me as we walk into the place, hand in hand.

"She is pregnant. We don't know how it happened..." I start to tell him over the howls and moans of the patient he already has on the table.

He arches a perfect eyebrow, crosses his blood stained arms and gives me a level stare.

"Well my Dabbler friend, I am on a limb going to go out and imagine it had to do with all of the sex that you two have been having. That will be one silver coin. Next patient please." He barks out while waving at the nurse on duty. She nods solemnly and hands him a bottle of vodka, from which he takes a healthy pull.

Yeah, his bedside manner could use a little work.

He hands the moaning Werewolf a Hello Kitty bandaid and a cheap sucker and shoos him away from the table as he beckons us towards it, once he realizes that despite his genius pronouncement, we aren't leaving.

Genevieve lets out a low moan of pain, soft, really barely noticeable and all of a sudden the drunken little shit is all business.

Gently he lowers her onto the table and pats her arm softly as she settles in, he snaps his fingers and his assistant puts two pillows under her head.

He doesn't have an xray machine or CAT scan set up, instead he has to rely on his own talents and senses.

Closing his eyes, he holds one hand over her swollen abdomen and says a secret chant under his breath. I can feel the cool whisper of magic wash across the room and then fade away.

Letting out a shuddering breath, he touches her swollen belly once and smiles at her brightly. He turns to me and gives me a broad wink.

"Congratulations! She is with child."

Because I am a reasonably mature adult, I refrain from breaking his large nose.

I am cool like that.

"Brilliant, I am pretty sure that we mentioned that on the way in Doc." I tell him through clenched teeth.

He nods wisely and pulls a small airline sized bottle of scotch from his lab coat pocket and slams it down. Tossing it over his shoulder, he crosses his arms in front of him and gives me a shrug.

"Please to excuse if I state the obvious. I do not know what else to tell you, do you maybe need me to explain bees and birds?" He asks sardonicly.

Losing patience, Marcus steps between us and picks the doctor up by his lapels and gives him an unfriendly shake.

"She wasn't showing any signs of pregnancy a few hours ago you fool. Examine her and tell us what the hell is going on." Marcus demands as he drops Greg ungently back down.

"Well that is weird then, is it not? Okey dokey, I will take another look see." He says cheerfully.

He lays one hand gently on her forehead and the other on her stomach and closes his eyes. Letting out a
81

long slow breath, he pulls the ragged crazy quilt of power that he has to him and tries to focus it on his patient.

After a long minute, he steps away from her and leans unsteadily against a handwashing station.

"I know not what to tell you fellows, she is not human or really any identifiable form of Sub Rosa. For all me know, this rapid state of developing preganacy, is more or less like normal for her. Best guess? She is hours away from giving birth, how many hours I no can say." He snaps his fingers again and the nurse doses him with vodka once more.

"It isn't possible." Genevieve says weakly from the examination table, her hand reaches out blindly seeking my own.

I move quickly to make sure that it finds it and I give her hand a reassuring squeeze.

"Shh, we will figure it out love." I bend down and whisper in her ear.

"No, you don't understand. I was careful, I knew what to do to make sure this never happened. It just isn't possible, there is no way I would have promised…" She starts to tell me. There is weakness and urgency in her voice and they both alarm me in more or less equal measure.

A chill hits me as my brain begins to connect some very unpleasant dots.

"Promise what?" I ask her flatly.

"Forgive me Robert Jones, what I have done, I did out of my love for you. I only promised what I did because I was so sure that it was impossible. I am so afraid now, this can't be happening." There is desperation, terror and sorrow in her voice, that finishes connecting the dots for me.

"No." Marcus says softly under his breath, as he also works out what she is talking about.

"What did you promise?" I ask her with a sick feeling in my gut that comes from already knowing the answer.

Before she can stop sobbing and answer, the lights all go out and the temperature drops a good twenty degrees, as the scent of brimstone fills the air.

Chumley comes in and winks at me obscenely, beforing leaning against the wall by the door as he holds it open for his master.

Lucifer strolls in clapping his school girl hands gleefully.

"Oh come now Dabbler, surely you have worked it out by now? I mean, how dumb can one guy be?" He sneers.

Chumley giggles and the sound of it will haunt me for the rest of my life.

"She promised me her first born son."

Marcus steps between the devil and my love, and after another pull from the bottle, the doctor shrugs and takes up station as well.

I stand up and turn to face the bastard and everyone in the room is pulling power to themselves. All of us as best we can, with the gifts that have been allowed to us. Some more than others, some less, but all of us standing together.

"Over my dead body." I growl at him.

"Well, hell yeah, that was pretty much always the plan." The Japanese school girl form wavers for a moment and the beast dwelling within is briefly revealed.

Chumley steps away from the wall with a grin suddenly full of way too many really sharp looking teeth. He takes a step towards me as his hand erupt into wicked claws.

From somewhere outside comes the sudden cawing of ravens.

Chapter Fifteen

Time stops.

Well, for everyone, but me it seems.

Everyone else is frozen in place, I can see the demonic glee on Lucifer's face and on the face of his servant. I can see the brave and hopeless determination on my best friend's face, as he prepares to die trying to protect my love.

I can see the, oh what the fuck let's do this expression on the doc's face, he has lived so long, that he really doesn't give a fuck how all this turns out. He will protect his patient or he will be destroyed trying.

Genevieve is frozen on the exam table, her beautiful face contorted by terror and desperation.

I look at her and take the time that whatever this force is giving me, to acknowledge my rage at her for not telling me what she did and to swallow that all down and use my love for her, to forgive her.

Nowhere as easy as it sounds, but love conquers all, haven't you fucking heard?

I forgive her, because that is what I have to do to keep on loving her and have her keep on loving me.

No time to dwell on it anyway, I have a more or less hopeless battle to fight against terrible odds.

She probably can't feel it, but I give her hand a squeeze, meant to communicate all that.

And just when you might think, hell shit can't get much weirder, well it just up and does.

Odin comes strolling into the room.

He looks just like I remember him.

Old dude dressed all in black with a black eyepatch over one eye. Shaggy mane of dirty blonde and gray hair and a long tangled beard.

"We need to talk." He says simply.

"Little busy." I tell him gesturing at the frozen mess all around us, part of me isn't accepting that any of this is real. I feel like an actor in a play that I auditioned for, drunk and now my lines are hard to come by, cause I missed all of the rehearsals.

He shakes his head ruefully and keeps walking towards me, as he walks, two ravens come into the room cawing loudly, until they each settle silently on his shoulders.

"I am Odin, we have all the time that we need to work this out, son." He tells me gravely,

My head is spinning from all that has happened, I have called my power to me with the understanding that whatever I can call, can't save us from the evil that is about to come at us. Hell, my power combined with my best friends isn't even close to enough. I have a new respect for Greg Smith, for standing with us, but his help isn't enough to tip the balance.

We are all probably going to die.

That thought should fill me with fear, instead I can feel a slow burning rage and lust for violence begin to fill me.

"Don't fight it boy, embrace the anger, use it to do what you need to do. I am going to tell you a story while you get good and pissed off." Odin says as he shrugs, sending the two ravens cawing back out of the room and into the night.

Power comes crashing into the room in an electrified dark wave, it washes past him and comes at me with a hunger that I can barely detect and don't understand.

"Long, long ago, the other Gods became angered at my son Loki and demanded his death. I fought against that choice as long as I could, until his actions left no other choice but to side with the other Gods and ordered his death. I found that I could not bear his utter destruction, so I used my power to steal away and hide a portion of his essense. I had to find a vessel that no God would look at twice, so I chose to hide it in the newborn offspring of a Warlock and human," His voice droned on in the background as the power filling the room found its target and began to fill me.

A scream builds silently in the back of my mind, as power begins to work its way into me. Every cell of my being, is being ripped apart and remade in the same pain wracked heartbeat.

"Time works differently between our realms, this was all long ago for me and mine, but I have taken the time to check in on you from time to time and you have made me proud. You have worked within the limits of what you apparently are and spit in the face of every foe. I have hidden what I left so carefully, that no Witch or Warlock or any other of our kind would ever detect it. I remove that concealment now and I am proud to call you, in a manner of speaking, a son of Odin." There is a wash of power in his voice now as he makes the proclamation.

And then the wave of power consumes me.

My little reserve of power, bigger since Marcus used his abilities to increase it, is snuffed out like a single candle in the face of a hurricane.

In its place, comes a sense of power without any real limits, at least none that my limited perceptions can understand.

It comes calmly, despite the rage that signaled its approach, it comes without ego, without lust for revenge or thirst for conquest. It comes as a simple offered tool to do what must be done, to save myself and those that I wish to protect.

It comes without the promise that it will be enough to do what needs to be done, it simply is power. I am free to use it as best I can, to do what I feel needs to be done.

Knowledge and skills flood into me too fast for me to make rational sense of, they are pushed aside to be made sense of later. That is, if we all survive long enough for their to be a later.

Jury is still out on that one.

I can feel the son of bitch in me now.

Loki, son of Odin. Trickster, devil, fool. Called many things. I am still me, but I can feel the first vauge stirrings of him inside me as well. If we survive this night, I will have to come to terms with his influence. I don't have a warm and fuzzy feeling that the process will be a smooth one.

Hell, I don't even have a warm and fuzzy feeling about surviving this night.

I can feel Loki's eagerness for the conflict to come, he doesn't care if we succeed in standing against Lucifer and his minion or not. He simply lusts for the thrill of the battle. Win or lose he just wants to kick a little ass.

For right now, that totally works for me.

The calmness fades and is replaced with a smouldering rage that only needs the slightest of kindle points to ignite, to explode.

"I must remove myself from this moment, this struggle my boy. I can not interfere any further in this matter. Use what has been given to you. Defend your lady love and your friends for now, if you survive this, we will move on to other challenges. Nod if you are ready for what is to come." His voice both booms and then fades as he prepares to take his leave.

I nod.

His faint smile of approval is the last I see of him, as he vanishes.

And then all fucking hell breaks loose.

Chapter Sixteen

Time starts up again.

Chumley comes at me with a horrible smile on his pale face. The smile falters a little, as I meet him halfway and grab him by his throat.

It fades completely as I tear his head off in one savage move.

I toss it overhand so it bounces off his Master's chest, leaving a bloody smear on the pristine looking uniform.

Kicking the servant's body out of the bloody way, I confront his Master, I can feel a manic grin spread across my face as I do so.

It scares me.

Even through the primalness of it, the joy I am taking in this fight, scares the shit out of me.

But not enough to stop.

I use some of my new found power to throw up a barrier between my love and my friends, who are protecting her.

Whatever this power is, nothing will harm them while I still stand.

Marcus is shouting at me, but I can't spare the time to listen just now, Genevieve is screaming, but sadly and shamefully, I can't spare the time for that now either. Greg Smith just smiles slightly and pulls out another little bottle of booze and slams it down. He smashes it against the far wall and waves his nurse to escape out of the back door.

She wastes no time in doing so.

Smart nurse.

"Well now, Dabbler. This is, I must admit, a bit of a shock. Still, I always thought there was more to you than met the eye. But all that aside, the Devil, as they say, is still in the details I fear." Lucifer blusters at me, in my heightened state of awareness, I can hear the shock in his otherwise calm sounding voice.

My only answer is a mindless challenging roar.

Have to fight against that.

For all my new found power, I still need to think, to be rational, not give into battle berserker rage. I need to find my way around whatever he throws at me.

I can sense that Marcus and the good doctor are attending to my lady love behind me. For now, I will use my strength to protect them, while they do so.

"Fuck off back to hell Lucifer. You will claim no souls this night." I growl at him, shocked at the power humming in my own voice.

Lucifer giggles coyley, hiding his mouth behind his hands.

I struggle against the impulse to wipe the giggle from his throat, by tearing it messily out, because I somehow sense that is what he wants me to try to do.

"Oh my little Dabbler friend, I can only remind you that despite your new found parentage and power, this has nothing to do with you. I have a signed contract between myself and your lovely lady and not even your new strength can change that. So, be a good little Demi God and give me that which is mine." Lucifer demands and I can taste the truth in his words.

"Take me instead." I blurt out without hesitation.

He actually flinches a little at the honesty of the offer.

"Not the deal I am afraid, so please step aside. Not looking for any trouble, just here to claim what is rightfully mine." He shakes a finger at me mockingly.

I throw a wave of power at him that actually knocks him a few steps backwards, sending him spinning into the wall behind him so hard, that I hear bones break.

"Ok then, we do this the hard fucking way." He says as he pulls himself back up to standing position.

Then he begins to rip all of the flesh off of his frame, piece by bloody piece, until the facade of the Japenese school girl is utterly gone and all that remains is an echo of the true form of the fallen Angel, who is forever banished to hell.

Heat floods into the room and the smell of burning brimstone becomes overpowering.

The Beast is truly terrible to look upon. Even just this barest spark of the demonic force he has sent to our world, should be mindnumbingly terrifying.

But like my daddy always told me......I am not smart enough to be afraid of anything.

"Bring it, you son of a bitch." I scream.

That is when Greg Smith steps effortlessly past all of my barrier's holding the swaddled form of the baby, that Genevieve just gave birth to.

"Please to excuse, but there is small complication that you should both be, well like, aware of, I suppose." He says gravely holding up the small wailing form.

"MINE!" The force of Lucifer's scream stuns me for a moment, even with my new powers. His voice drips tones of greed, perversion and rage that are too vast for me to fully comprehend.

A wave of fire and ash reach out to consume the doctor and his little patient, but they splash harmlessly off of both.

The doctor makes a show of coughing and clearing his throat before speaking again. He holds the baby with one arm while brushing ash off of himself with the other.

"Before I was, so very rudely interrupted, I was about to announce that, well, what the hell, let's end the fucking suspense, it is a girl child!" He cackles giving the Lord of Hell the finger.

There is a single moment of absolute silence.

Lucifer screams, yeah you can go ahead and add it to the ever increasing list of the worst sounds that I have ever heard list and launches himself towards the doctor and my daughter.

Not today Lucifer, yeah, not today.

I catch him by one curved horn as he goes by and fling him back the way he came. He slams into the far wall, hard, but gets up too fast for my comfort level.

In the end, I am not really fighting Satan at his full power, I am fighting the shred of power he sent out into our realm. Still, that power is staggering by any standards.

That being said.

I kick his ass.

Rage fuels the blows that I am raining down on him, that is too simple really. It isn't just rage, it is that and fear, fear of losing those I love, fear of failing to protect those that are mine to protect. Fear of not being strong enough to stop him. I smash at him harder with every blow and I can feel that which is Loki, urging me to keep smashing until there is nothing left to kill.

No.

No, not like this.

I will end this as me, not as some weird semi divine fragment of some ancient God.

"Enough, you have no claim here Lucifer. Begone now." I sigh as I stand over his battered form.

He looks up at me and I can see the shrewd calculations in his eyes, he will retreat and come back at us, another day.

I don't know if he can actually be destroyed, but that look makes me really want to give it my best shot.

"Well played little Dabbler, be warned now, you and yours just graduated to the top of my shit list. Not a place that any of you are likely to survive I fear." He smiles up at me.

My shoulders slump and a weariness washes over me, but before I can give in to weakness two ravens come swooping in to rest on my shoulders.

"Well Lucy, old pal. All that being said, I will trust on getting by with a little help from my friends." I tell him with a grin.

Then both birds flap away from me and poop on the bastards head for me before disappearing .

Yeah, it is the little things in life that count the most.

The Lord of Hell roars one last time and then vanishes, taking the headless corpse of his servant with him.

I stagger and catch myself on the edge of a table, before I fall on my ass. Sound rushes in again, I can hear my daughter crying.

I can also hear my love whispering comforts to her.

My best friend is standing next to them beaming at me, and I know that his happiness for us is real and genuine.

The doctor snaps his fingers a couple of times before he figures out that the nurse isn't coming back and that he will have to round up his own damn drink.

The battle, for the moment is over.

In the aftermath, part of me wants a cold beer.

And the other part, the part that I will have to somehow learn to deal with now, is demanding mead and wenches.

His tone is mercilessly sly and I instinctively know that I will have to guard against his influences.

Marcus solves the dilemenia for now, by walking over to the good doctor's fridge and grabbing both of us a cold beer.

Always have liked that guy.

I drink my cold beer, I shake both my best friend's hand and the doctors hand, before kneeling down by my love, who is cradling our daughter in her arms.

Then I kiss her and whisper my love and forgiveness into her ear, as I stroke the bald as a cueball head of my newborn child.

Trust me friends, human, Warlock, Dabbler or fucking Demi God.

It doesn't get better than that.

Chapter Seventeen

Odin and I stand just outside of one of the countless entrances to the underground tunnels that are controlled by the Goblins.

With my newfound awareness, I am aware of the disturbing hum of the what the Goblins call their "Great Machine" powering up.

The sound has a wrongness to it, that I am powerless to describe, think fingernails on a chalkboard, times infinity and beyond.

Then just to make it suck even more, add in some Kayne West.

Odin lays a hand on my shoulder and it serves to focus me on why we are here right now.

"You know what must be done." He says simply and then he steps away and leaves me to it.

I stand alone for a moment and contemplate what I am about to do, I can feel the formidable wards standing between me and the machine, that the Goblins have slaved away for centuries to build.

No bragging, but I also know that I can brush them aside, with a shrug of my will.

I wish that we could take the time to talk to the reclusive Goblins and explain why we can't allow them to do what their culture more or less demands that they do.

Whatever the hell that is.

But since we can't do that, I am here to use force to pull the plug and stop whatever it is that they are doing, before they bring flights of rabid Angels down upon our heads.

The hum of their machine is seductive, it pleads its case in its own way, to be allowed to finish the task with what it has been built for. Out of respect, I listen for a few moments before I do what I came here to do.

I bow my head and I broadcast an apology for what I am about to do, even as I gather the power I need to do it.

Odin smiles encouragingly and stands slightly away from me, guarding my back as I savor the sweet rush of power that I gather into a simple shape.

His smile broadens as I fling that shape towards The Great Machine of the Goblins.

I keep adding terrible sounds to my list of terrible sounds, the sounds that will haunt me to my dying day.

The awful wail of Goblin voices, following the magical monkey wrench I threw into the workings of their Great Machine, just pushed itself to the top of that damn list.

My life is so weird now, now that I am unsure what God I should ask for forgiveness.

Mission accomplished, well at least for now anyway, This will slow down whatever it is that they are trying to do, but it will not end it. I have bought us some time, but that doesn't mean that I have to feel good about it.

Oddly Odin's approving smack on my back, doesn't make me feel any better.

Loki enjoyed the show anyway.

Yeah, we aren't going to be besties.

I look up into the sky with my newly enhanced vision and as I watch, all of the flights of Angels peel off and go to wherever they keep themselves.

 For now, we will call that a win.

Chapter Eighteen

I have a daughter.

Fuck me gently with a chainsaw.

Her name is Pyper.

I had no input into that particular choice, by the way.

Her mother informed me that it was traditional amongst her kind, that the mother got to choose the name of the child.

This could, of course be total bullshit, but in the interest of domestic harmony, I have made the choice to go with it.

Call it being supportive.

Call it diplomacy.

Call it utter cowardice.

Don't really care what you call it, because I love this little person, no matter what her name is, in a way that I never even dreamed was possible.

We brought her cuteness to the Librarian and he did a few tests, that he was obnoxious enough to refuse to share the results of.

It took some of the sting out it that he couldn't hide the smile on his face, as he talked to us about it.

Always have liked that guy.

Dominique has returned to his pack, he still hates me, but that hatred is tempered at least a little now, by a little gratitude for what we did for him. He asked for no explanation when we returned home with a baby and we offered him none. Before he left, he leaned forward and sniffed at me.

He then looked at me with something almost like respect, before leaving without a word.

The Packmaster isn't a friend, he isn't an ally, but maybe at least now, he isn't a mortal enemy and sometimes that is just as good as it gets.

The Council, still led by Helena Regret, hasn't approached me yet, but that day is coming. They will want to understand what happened to me and what I am now.

Good luck with that, because I sure as hell don't understand it myself.

They will be summoning me to appear before them soon, if I was still just a Dabbler, they would have done so by now.

But I am not just a Dabbler anymore, so they are proceeding cautiously for the moment.

It is hot tonight, so we have taken the stairs to the doorway that we aren't supposed to have keys to and we are all hanging out on the roof. Classic rock is playing softly on a battered boom box.

My best friend is rocking the cradle with one foot absently, while he pours over magical tomes trying hard to understand what has happened to his best friend. My daughter coos at him while he does so.

Figures.

Even newborn girls love him .

Meanwhile I am dancing with my lady love, I whisper some words into the night and suddenely we are floating a few feet above the roof top, spinning in slow lazy circles.

Together we dance.

The Puppet whispered seven words to me before she died.

Want to know what the hell they were?

Of course you do.

Well then, here the fuck they are boys and girls.

These are the words that I will share, as I take my lady love into my arms and rise to float above this city we are bound to and call home.

These then are the seven words that I whisper into my love's ear.

Seven words.

Life Is Short, Always Remember To Dance.

Remember them well and whisper them to others, whenever you can.

The End.

I started writing this book over a year ago, I opened it with an active shooter event long before such an event tragically came to pass in Las Vegas. Friends urged me to rewrite the beginning of this book and I seriously considered doing so, for awhile. I came to the decision not to, because to change it would alter the course of the plot too much. Please know that I am no way glorifying the violence that has tragically changed the way we perceive Las Vegas, our hearts go out to all affected by the events that took place on that sad and horrible day.

This book has caught our own personal lives in a state of flux, by the time you read this, we will have relocated our household some one hundred and thirty miles away to Ocean Shores, Washington. We have rolled the dice and decided to semi retire here, because from our first visit we fell in love with the place. It would be really helpful if everyone bought lots and lots of our books to help out with the whole semi retiring bit, lol.

So stay tuned friends, more books and more changes coming your way soon. We appreciate each and every one of you readers, you are why we do this thing that we do. Whatever changes in our personal lives, you remain the reason we do what we do. If you see us at a show, please do not hesitate to come talk to us, we love our fans!

The usual thank yous go out to the usual suspects, you all know who you are by now. Rita Ohara, you kick serious ass and you are the only person I have ever co written a story with. Micheal Ohara, your taste in beer is questionable, but you rock as a human being.

As always a big thank you to my talented and tireless editor, who also happens to be my lovely wife. You are tasked with the thankless job on making my writing shine, as you wade through the manuscript red pen in hand..

We hope you enjoyed book two of the Dabbler series, give us your input at alucardpress@yahoo.com. It is an understatement to say that we love hearing from fans.

Turn the page for a hint at what is to come for this series…

GODS OF SIN CITY

I took my daughter to her first day of daycare today, she is two years old now in human years. My powers are dialed down and I make calm chitchat with the young blonde female at the front desk.

Pyper holds my hand as we fill out the required paperwork, she is on her best behavior.

Which makes me really fucking nervous.

I can feel her voice in my mind asking me endless questions, as her solemn green eyes take in her surroundings.

The woman behind the desk smiles at us blandly, as she goes about the business of signing us up. Her normalcy makes me wonder how good of an idea this is, but I have been outvoted.

Marcus and Genevieve think that it is a good idea to expose her to the normalcy of the human world.

I remain unconvinced.

Things have been quiet since we slapped down the Devil himself and defeated his attempt at claiming our child.

Too quiet.

We keep waiting for the other foot to drop, so to speak.

On more than one front.

The Goblins never acknowlededged what we did to stop their progress on what they call their Great Machine. They simply started building it again. The Angels have retreated to their realm and steadfastly ignore us now.

I am ok with that.

Lucifer hasn't taken a new form yet to come back to Vegas to vex us.

I am more than ok with that.

Pyper is a blonde little bundle of joyful energy and hasn't displayed anything like magical ability or powers yet, aside from a weak telepathic connection between her and I, but we know that it is coming.

And if we know that, so do other players in this game.

Those players will have to get past me.

And while that may not be impossible, it is for some complicated reasons a bit harder than it used to be.

To those who want to test that level of difficulty.

The ghost of Loki and I agree on one thing.

Bring it bitches.

The End

www.ingramcontent.com/pod-product-compliance
Lightning Source LLC
Chambersburg PA
CBHW070459130626
46555CB00003B/1068